Vincent Paints His House

TEDD ARNOLD

Holiday House / New York

For Jeanie and Henri

Printed and bound in November 2020 at Toppan Leefung, DongGuan City, China.
The artwork was rendered digitally using Photoshop software.
www.holidayhouse.com
7 9 10 8

Library of Congress Cataloging-in-Publication Data
Arnold, Tedd, author, illustrator.
Vincent paints his house / by Tedd Arnold. — First edition.
Summary: Vincent's animal friends disagree on how he should
paint his house, so Vincent comes up with a colorful solution.
ISBN 978-0-8234-3210-3 (hardcover)
[1. House painting—Fiction. 2. Color—Fiction. 3. Animals—Fiction.] I. Title.
PZ7.A7379Vi 2015
[E]—dc23
2014006045

ISBN 978-0-8234-3686-6 (paperback)

Time to paint the house!

"Hmm . . . ,"
said Vincent.

Vincent could not decide what color to use.

"Maybe I will just paint it white," said Vincent.

"White is nice," said Vincent.

"Stop!" said the spider. "This is MY house, and I like red."

"Stop!" said the caterpillar. "This is MY house, and I like yellow."

"Stop!" said the beetle. "This is MY house, and I like purple."

"Stop!" said the bird. "This is MY house, and I like blue."

"Blue is nice," said Vincent.

"Stop!" said the snake. "This is MY house, and I like green."

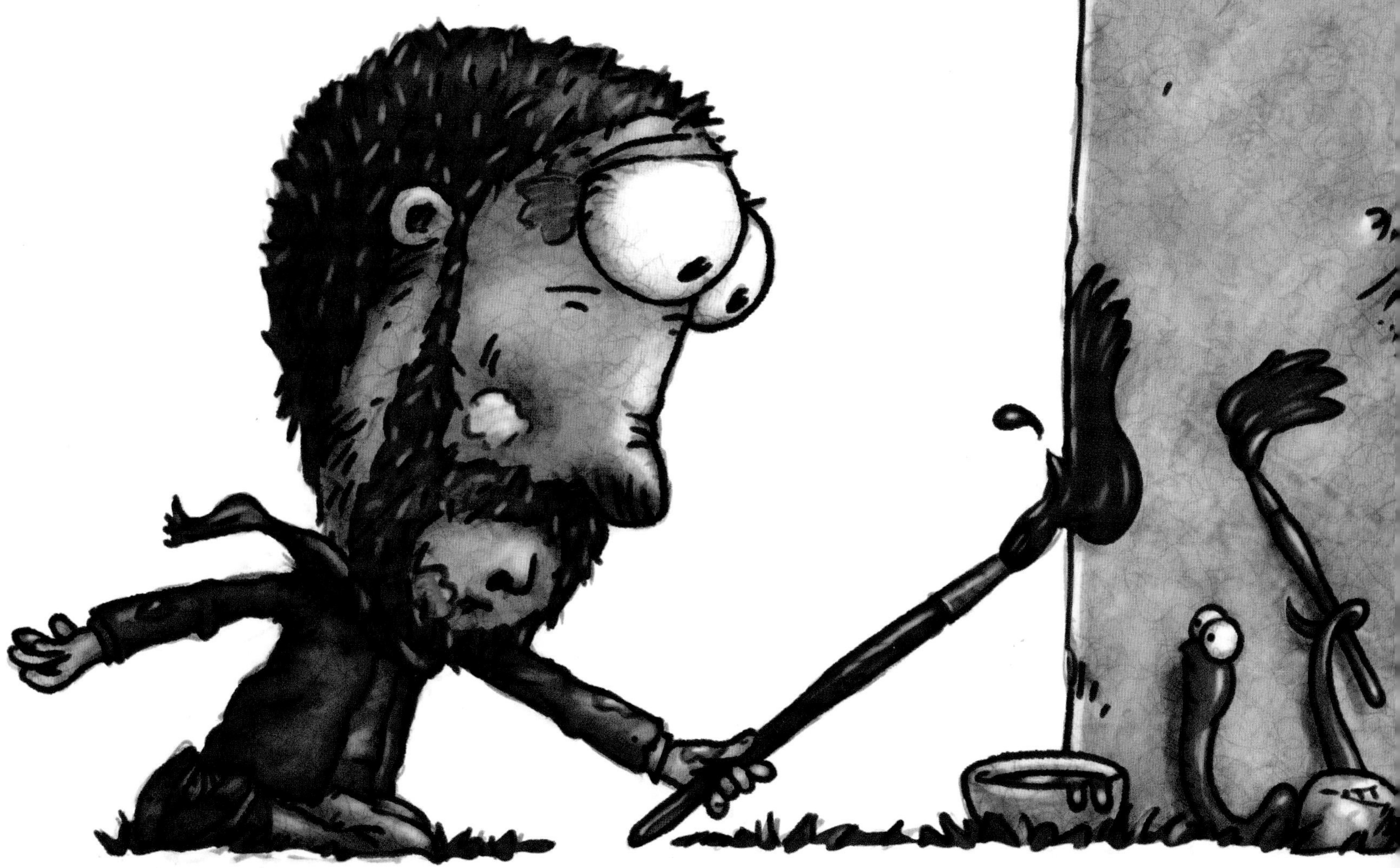

"Stop!" said the mouse. "This is MY house, and I like brown."

"Brown is nice," said Vincent.

"Stop!" said the bat. "This is MY house, and I like black."

"Black is nice," said Vincent,

"but actually,
this is
my house!"

Everyone was happy!

The End